THE DRAGONSITTER
to the Rescue

THE DRAGONSITTER to the Rescue

Josh Lacey

Illustrated by Garry Parsons

LITTLE, BROWN AND COMPANY
New York • Boston

Little, Brown and Company
Hachette Book Group
1290 Avenue of the Americas, New York, NY 10104
Visit us at lb-kids.com

Originally published in 2016 by Andersen Press Limited in Great Britain
First U.S. Edition: March 2017

Little, Brown and Company is a division of Hachette Book Group, Inc.
The Little, Brown name and logo are trademarks of Hachette Book Group, Inc.

The publisher is not responsible for websites (or their content) that are not owned by the publisher.

Library of Congress Control Number: 2016956913

ISBNs: 978-0-316-38244-1 (hardcover), 978-0-316-29916-9 (trade paperback), 978-0-316-29917-6 (ebook)

Printed in the United States of America

LSC-C

10 9 8 7 6 5 4 3 2 1

THE DRAGONSITTER
to the Rescue

From: Edward Smith-Pickle

To: Morton Pickle

Date: Saturday, April 15

Subject: We've arrived!

Attachments: View; That's my bed!

Dear Uncle Morton,

Here is the view from our hotel window. If you look very closely, you can see Big Ben.

As you can also see, your dragons are fine. They both had a good dinner. Now they're fast asleep.

Dad didn't actually want to bring them. He asked Mom to take them to Paris, but she said, "No way." She said she didn't want two badly behaved dragons spoiling her romantic weekend with Gordon.

Dad said wasn't a romantic weekend in Paris a bit of a cliché, and Mom said she'd rather have a cliché than nothing at all, which was all *he* used to give her.

Gordon looked really embarrassed while they were shouting at one another, but Emily and I didn't mind. We're used to it.

Mom won. So the dragons are here. I have brought the egg, too, just in case it hatches. I wouldn't want a new dragon to arrive in an empty house.

I have to go now. Dad says it's bedtime. First thing tomorrow morning we're visiting the Natural History Museum.

Emily wants to go on the London Eye instead, but Dad says we'll do that the day after.

I hope you're having fun in Tibet. Have you seen the yeti yet?

Love,

Eddie

Dear Uncle Morton,

I have to tell you some bad news.

We have lost Arthur.

He's somewhere in London, but I don't know where.

Today, we went to the Natural History Museum. I've always wanted to go there, so I was *really* excited.

The only problem was Dad said the dragons had to stay in the hotel without us.

I said that was very unfair, but Dad said he wanted to spend some quality time with his children, not a pair of fire-breathing lizards. He said we could take them to a park later if they needed to stretch their wings.

He absolutely, definitely, no-question-about-it refused to change his mind.

So I hid Arthur in my backpack.

I knew I shouldn't have, but I couldn't stop myself.

I told him to be quiet in there. He *was*, on the subway. Very. And he carried on being quiet in

the café where we stopped for a morning snack. I dropped some croissant through the top of the backpack, which seemed to keep him happy.

He even stayed quiet in the museum. He didn't make a squeak while we looked at the birds and the bears and the earthworms and the giraffe and the rhino and the dodo and the dolphin and the blue whale.

But when we got to the T. rex, he wriggled out of my backpack and flew off to have a look. Maybe he thought it was a long-lost cousin.

He flew the entire length of the T. rex from tail to head and landed on its nostrils. People were pointing and shouting and taking pictures.

Dad asked, "Where did that come from?"

I pretended I didn't know.

Guards came running. One of them said, "You're not allowed to have flying toys inside the museum."

I explained, "He's not a toy. He's a dragon."

The guard said he didn't care what it was, I just had to get it out of here right now, this minute, before he called the police and had us all thrown out for making a public nuisance of ourselves.

I said I would if I could catch him.

The guard got on his walkie-talkie and called for reinforcements.

Unfortunately, catching Arthur was easier
said than done. He jumped off the T. rex and
whooshed over our heads, waggling his wings.

I ran after him. So did Dad and Emily and lots of
guards.

Arthur was faster than any of us. He flew along
the corridors, looped the loop around some
statues, dive-bombed a crowd of Japanese
tourists, and disappeared through the revolving

doors. By the time we got outside, he had vanished.

We searched for hours, but we couldn't find him anywhere.

I wanted to keep on looking all night, but Dad said we'd just be wasting our time. So we came back to the hotel.

Ziggy was fast asleep. She still is. I don't know what I'm going to say to her when she wakes up.

Dad says if I was so concerned about the dragons, I shouldn't have hidden Arthur in my backpack in the first place. I suppose he's right.

I'm really sorry, Uncle Morton.

This whole thing is my fault, and I wish I knew how to make it better.

Eddie

Dear Uncle Morton,

I'm very sorry, but I've got some more bad news.

I've lost your other dragon, too.

Emily and I were brushing our teeth in the bathroom when we heard a terrible noise coming from the bedroom.

We rushed out of the bathroom and found Ziggy going wild. She was trying to break through the windows and get onto the balcony. She must have realized Arthur had gone missing.

Dad was standing on his bed, holding a pillow. He yelled at me to do something.

I didn't want to let her out, but there really wasn't any choice. One more minute and she would have smashed the whole place to pieces.

So I opened the door.

Ziggy charged onto the balcony, flapped her wings, and took off.

A moment later, she'd disappeared into the night.

I feel awful. I can't believe I've lost both your dragons. I wish I knew how to find them.

Do you have any brilliant ideas?

Dad says there's no point in writing to you because you won't be checking your e-mails in Tibet, but I hope you get this message.

Please write back if you do.

Eddie

From: Edward Smith-Pickle

To: Morton Pickle

Date: Monday, April 17

Subject: 8,000,000

Attachments: Londoners

Dear Uncle Morton,

Your dragons are still missing.

We spent the whole day walking around London, but we didn't see any sign of them.

This city is so big!

Dad says eight million people live here. I think we met most of them.

I asked everyone if they'd seen a missing dragon. Some of them laughed. Others just walked past as if they couldn't even hear me.

People who live in London are quite rude. Dad says it's the same in all big cities. Emily wanted to know if Paris is like this, too, and Dad said it's even worse.

I hope Mom and Gordon are having more fun than us.

Love,

Eddie

Dear Uncle Morton,

We spent today searching for your dragons again, but we still haven't found them.

Dad says not to worry—they'll come back in their own good time.

He says this is our one chance to spend a few days in London and we should be making the most of it, missing dragons or no missing dragons.

But I don't want to make the most of it. I just want to find Ziggy and Arthur.

Eddie

From: Morton Pickle

To: Edward Smith-Pickle

Date: Tuesday, April 18

Subject: Re: Still missing

Dear Eddie,

I have just seen your messages. The internet is a rare treat here in Tibet, but I managed to check my e-mails on a sherpa's phone.

Thank you for letting me know about the dragons.

You need not worry about Ziggy. She will be perfectly safe. Dragons are wise creatures, and she is even more sensible than most. She also has strong wings and powerful claws. I can't imagine anyone or anything in London will be a threat to her.

However, Arthur is quite different, and I am very concerned for his safety. A small dragon is not safe alone in a big city. He might have been run over or kidnapped or suffered some even more horrible fate.

I suggest you call the police and ask for their help.

I do hope you find them both soon, so you can enjoy your vacation in London. I have fond memories of the years I spent in that vast gray town. Few places could be more different than my current location: a cold, snow-covered mountainside in a remote region of Tibet.

We have had no confirmed sightings of the yeti, but I have arranged a meeting with a local shaman tomorrow, and I am hoping he will bring good news.

With love from your affectionate uncle,

Morton

Dear Uncle Morton,

I did what you suggested.

I called the police and told them we had lost a dragon in the Natural History Museum.

First, the police officer thought I was joking.

Then he said he would arrest me for wasting police time.

Do you have any other suggestions for finding Arthur?

Eddie

Dear Uncle Morton,

Your dragons are still missing.

Dad says he's had quite enough of them, even if they're not here anymore, and we should just concentrate on enjoying what little time we have left in London.

But I can't make the most of anything because I'm too worried about Ziggy and Arthur.

I made some posters and pinned them to trees.

No one has replied yet, but I hope they will soon.

Love,

Eddie

Have you seen
this dragon?

He is small and green.

He has two wings and smoke
coming out of his nostrils.

He was last seen on Sunday, April 16
in the Natural History Museum.

If you see him, please contact Eddie.

edwardsmithpickle@gmail.com

From: Edward Smith-Pickle

To: Morton Pickle

Date: Thursday, April 20

Subject: Noodles

Attachments: Gerrard Street

Dear Uncle Morton,

We have been looking for your dragons again today.

We didn't find them.

We did see some other dragons, but not yours.

Dad's friend Julie came to have lunch with us. She's really pretty, like all his girlfriends.

Dad said she's not actually his girlfriend, but fingers crossed. I hope she will be. She was very nice.

Also she knows a lot about dragons.

She took us to Chinatown because she said they

have hundreds of dragons there. She was right.
There were dragons everywhere.

Unfortunately, none of them were Arthur or
Ziggy. But we did have some delicious noodles.

I put up some more posters. I still haven't gotten
any replies.

Love,

Eddie

From: Edward Smith-Pickle

To: Morton Pickle

Date: Friday, April 21

Subject: She's back!

Attachments: A very tired dragon

Dear Uncle Morton,

I have some good news and some bad news.

The good news is Ziggy is back.

The bad news is Arthur isn't.

Ziggy must have arrived in the middle of the night. She's asleep on the balcony. I suppose she was exhausted from searching so much. In a minute I'm going to wake her up to say hello. Then we're going to spend the day searching for Arthur. Julie is going to come with us. She's taken the day off work.

24

Dad asked if we could do something more interesting than looking for Arthur. But I said we've got to find him.

Also, Julie won't mind. She loves dragons. She told me so yesterday.

Emily said maybe we would be able to see Arthur from the top of the London Eye, but I know she didn't really mean it. She just wants to go up there herself.

I told her there would be time to enjoy ourselves after we've found him.

Love,

Eddie

From: Edward Smith-Pickle

To: Morton Pickle

Date: Friday, April 21

Subject: Fizz

📎 **Attachments:** Cheers!; Shower

Dear Uncle Morton,

We are cold and wet and homeless, and it's all your dragon's fault.

We spent today searching for Arthur, but we didn't find him.

Julie took us to Covent Garden and Trafalgar Square and the National Gallery, which were all very nice, but I didn't enjoy them very much because I was too worried about Arthur.

So Dad said tonight, as a special treat to cheer ourselves up, we could order room service and watch a movie in bed. He invited Julie to join us, but she was busy.

Once we got back to the hotel, Emily and I took a bath and put on our PJs, then switched on the TV. Dad ordered burgers and fries, plus lemonade for me, orange juice for Emily, and a bottle of red wine for him.

I wanted to get a drink for Ziggy, but Dad said she'd be fine with water.

We had just started watching the movie when the waiter arrived with our dinner on a big, silver tray.

Dad poured himself a big drink and stretched out on the bed and said, "Cheers." We all clinked glasses.

I felt a bit guilty about Arthur. You know how much he loves fries. Also, I didn't like having fun while he was missing. Dad told me not to worry.

He said, "Look at Ziggy. She's enjoying herself, isn't she?" And he was right. She was.

She ate her burger in one gulp, and her fries in another. Then she ate most of mine, too.

Unfortunately, she also drank my lemonade.

I didn't see her doing it, but she must have swallowed the whole thing because suddenly she gave an enormous burp.

Flames shot across the room. A corner of the quilt caught fire.

Dad jumped off the bed and grabbed the fire extinguisher. He was just figuring out how to turn it on when the fire alarm went off.

It was the loudest noise I've ever heard. Until Emily screamed.

Ziggy didn't seem too bothered by all the fuss. She just reached across the bed and grabbed the remains of our burgers.

I was suggesting everyone should calm down when the sprinklers started. It was like standing under a waterfall. In seconds we were all soaked.

Now we're waiting in the parking lot in our wet pajamas while the firemen check all the rooms.

Dad is talking to the people who own the hotel. They want us to leave immediately, but we don't have anywhere to go.

Dad says the whole thing is your stupid dragon's fault and if you had a scrap of decency you'd come straight back from Tibet and look after her yourself.

I thought you probably couldn't do that, Uncle Morton.

But do you think maybe you could?

Eddie

Dear Uncle Morton,

Don't worry about coming back from Tibet. Everything is fine. We're in a new hotel.

It's quite nice here. The TV in the room is even bigger than the last one, and they left two free chocolates on our pillows.

Ziggy seems to like it, too. She ate both the chocolates, then fell asleep on the carpet.

I don't know why she isn't more worried about Arthur. Perhaps she's forgotten all about him. Dad said some mothers are like that.

She's actually very lucky to be here at all. There was a big sign outside the hotel that said NO PETS ALLOWED.

Dad asked if they could make an exception for dragons.

They laughed and said dragons could stay free of charge, which was very nice of them.

They tried to change their minds when they saw Ziggy, but Dad said a deal is a deal, so they let us all in.

There's only one problem. Arthur doesn't know where we are. If he goes to the other hotel, he won't be able to find us.

Do you think I should go back there and wait for him?

Eddie

Dear Uncle Morton,

Today is our last day in London.

We're going home tomorrow.

There's still no sign of Arthur.

I want to stay here until we find him, but Dad says that's just not possible. Apparently this hotel is costing him "an arm and a leg." Also, we have school next week, and he has to go back to Wales.

Dad asked us how would we like to spend our last day in London.

I said I wanted to look for Arthur. Emily said she wanted to go on the London Eye.

Dad said we've been looking for Arthur every day this week and it was about time we did something a bit more interesting. So we're going to the London Eye.

Apparently Julie has never been on it, even though she's lived in London her whole life.

Emily can't stop smiling. I don't know why. Doesn't she even care about your dragon?

I can't believe we're wasting our last day sightseeing when we could be looking for Arthur.

But everyone is ignoring me.

Eddie

Dear Uncle Morton,

We have found Arthur!

Well, we've almost found him.

We know where he is, anyway.

Today, we went on the London Eye. I didn't really want to be there, but it was actually quite amazing. From the top we could see the whole city.

I looked in every direction, but I couldn't see any dragons.

When we came down again, Julie had a chat with one of the guards, who suggested we try the

Lost Property Office at Baker Street Station. He said lost things in London often end up there.

He was right!

We took the subway to Baker Street and talked to the duty officer at the Lost Property Office. He said maybe he could help us.

He looked through his files and pulled out a piece of paper and said, "Does this sound like what you're looking for?"

Unfortunately, Arthur wasn't there anymore. He's been taken away by the Westminster Animal Rescue Service.

Dad said they're welcome to keep him. But he was only joking.

We're going there now to get him back.

Eddie

LOST PROPERTY REPORT

Lost Property Office, Baker Street Station

Item

One creature. Species unknown. Small, green, possibly dangerous.

Location

The item was found on a Circle Line subway train traveling clockwise between Gloucester Road and High Street Kensington.

Description

At approximately 8 p.m. last night, a passenger boarded a Circle Line train at Gloucester Road and noticed the item on the next seat. The carriage was not crowded, and there was no sign of an owner nearby.

The passenger alerted a member of staff, who summoned the British Transport Police. They placed the item in a cardboard box and brought it to the Lost Property Office at Baker Street.

The Duty Officer examined the creature, but could not find a collar or any evidence of a microchip.

However, the creature does possess very sharp teeth, which it has already used to bite two Transport for London staff members. Luckily, both of them were wearing thick boots.

The Lost Property Office has very limited resources for livestock or pets, so the Duty Officer placed the item in the Umbrella Room for safekeeping.

I have reported the matter to the Westminster Animal Rescue Service. I hope they will arrive soon. The item has already destroyed six umbrellas and is currently working its way through a seventh.

Andy Malik

Andy Malik, Deputy Duty Officer, Baker Street Lost Property Office

Dear Uncle Morton,

The Westminster Animal Rescue Service doesn't have Arthur anymore. They've taken him to the zoo.

We're on our way.

Love,

Eddie

The Westminster Animal Rescue Service

Report by Monika Pielowska, Senior Warden

I was contacted by the Deputy Duty Officer in Baker Street Station, who informed me of a situation at the Transport for London Lost Property Office. I was at an address nearby, so I made my way directly to Baker Street.

The Duty Officer told me that a small creature, species unknown, was handed in last night and placed in the Umbrella Room.

The Duty Officer claimed that the creature was extremely dangerous, although it seemed perfectly harmless to me.

The creature does have very sharp teeth and an unusual habit of breathing smoke through its nostrils.

One of the Duty Officers suggested it might be a dragon, but I assured him that such things do not exist. I am not an expert on lizards, but it looks like an overgrown newt to me.

Whatever it might be, the creature was clearly very hungry. It had already tried to eat every umbrella in the place, without much success. So I lured it into a cage with a bait of raw steak.

Once it was safely locked inside the cage, I carried the creature to my van and brought it to London Zoo, where it will be properly identified by an expert.

From: Edward Smith-Pickle

To: Morton Pickle

Date: Saturday, April 22

Subject: Proof

Attachments: Zoo Admission Sheet

Dear Uncle Morton,

We've found Arthur! He's in the zoo.

The only problem is they won't let him go.

They want proof we are his registered owners. Do you have any proof, Uncle Morton?

If so, please send it to us ASAP. Otherwise, Arthur will be sent to another zoo for tests, and then how are we supposed to get him back?

Love,

Eddie

The Zoological Society of London

NEW ADMISSION INFORMATION SHEET

Species: Unknown.

Habitat: Unknown.

Diet: Unknown.

Sex: Unknown.

Age: Unknown.

Previous owner: Unknown.

Place of origin: the Circle Line.

Notes: Three of our foremost lizard experts have examined this unusual creature, trying to determine its species, but they remain baffled.

One of them suggested it may be a rare form of the Jamaican chameleon. Another has agreed to consult his colleagues at the Taronga Zoo in Sydney. The third suffered minor burns and is currently in the emergency room of the Royal Free Hospital. The creature has not been disturbed again.

It will be tranquilized on Monday morning and transferred to Whipsnade Zoo for further examination.

Dear Uncle Morton,

Don't worry about sending the proof. We've got Arthur. We rescued him ourselves.

Actually, Ziggy did. She was amazing!

We were supposed to be going straight home today, but I asked if we go to the zoo on our way, and Dad said if we had to.

I think he was just sad because Julie isn't coming with us. She went to have Sunday lunch with her mom and dad in Ipswich, and we weren't invited.

Dad doesn't know when he's going to see her again.

I asked why doesn't he invite her to stay in Wales, and he said maybe he will.

Anyway, we packed our bags and checked out of the hotel. They gave us some more chocolates as a going-home present. Then Dad drove us to the zoo.

It's in the middle of a nice park. That was where Dad made us wait while he talked to whoever was in charge.

We had to promise not to move an inch. And we didn't. While Dad went into the zoo, we sat on the grass, eating chocolates.

Suddenly, Ziggy lifted her head into the air and looked around. Somehow she must have sensed Arthur was nearby.

She flapped her wings.

Faster and faster.

Just before she took off, I jumped on her back.

Emily was shouting at me to get off. She grabbed Ziggy's tail and clung on.

With one shake, Ziggy sent her flying across the grass. Then she flapped her wings again and we were in the air.

All around the park I could see people shouting and pointing at us. I wanted to wave back, but I knew what would happen if I let go.

The zoo is surrounded by a huge metal fence covered with spikes and barbed wire. That didn't stop Ziggy. She just flew over the top and swept past the cages.

The animals went wild.

Parrots shrieked. Monkeys screamed. The lions threw back their heads and roared, telling us to get lost.

Only the gorillas wanted to stand and fight.

They ran across the grass and into the middle of their enclosure, then beat their fists against their chests.

Ziggy ignored them all. She just flew this way and that, following her nose, searching for Arthur.

Suddenly, she flipped around in midair and headed for some gray buildings at the back of the zoo where visitors aren't even allowed.

Ziggy seemed to know exactly where she was going. She flew straight toward a big window on the fifth floor. On the other side of the glass, I could see a room filled with about twenty cages, each of them holding a different animal. There was a monkey and a chimp and a wolf and a marmoset and a goose and a small dragon, all going wild, beating their paws and their claws against the bars.

Ziggy breathed a great gust of fire and the glass exploded. Another gust and the bars melted on half the cages.

The wolf howled. The monkey lost his eyebrows. The goose almost went up in flames.

Arthur took off. He sped across the floor and through the window, his little wings flapping like

a hummingbird's. Then he landed beside me on his mom's back.

Through the window, I could see a zookeeper staring at us, his mouth wide open, his clothes smoking.

I wanted to say sorry, but there wasn't time before Ziggy whirled around and flew across the zoo.

The gorillas went wild again. The lions roared. I could see all the penguins staring up at us, and the giraffes, too. I would have liked to dive down and have a better look, but Ziggy wanted to get out of there ASAP.

She soared over the fence and plunged down to land on the grass beside Emily.

Dad was already running toward us. He must have seen what was happening. He bundled us into the car, and we drove straight home.

When we got here, Arthur ate seven hot dogs, two baked potatoes, and half a bar of chocolate, then fell asleep in front of the TV.

I think he's going to be fine.

Dad has gone back to Wales. He says next time he'd rather it was just us and no dragons. Maybe they could stay with Mom and Gordon instead.

Love,

Eddie

From: Morton Pickle

To: Edward Smith–Pickle

Date: Monday, April 24

Subject: Re: The Zoo

Dear Eddie,

What wonderful news about Arthur!

Congratulations on rescuing him from the zoo. It's actually extremely fortunate that you did, because I don't have any proof that I own him.

In fact, I don't own him. Nor do I own Ziggy. Dragons are not like dogs, cats, gerbils, or any other ordinary pet. They cannot really have an owner because they own themselves. Ziggy and Arthur are simply staying with me until they decide to move elsewhere.

All is well here in Tibet. I am currently staying in a village high in the Himalayas. We still do not have a confirmed sighting of the yeti, but today we did find what might have been one of his footprints in the snow. We are going to search for him again first thing tomorrow morning.

I'm so pleased that the dragons are in such good hands while I'm away. Thanks again for looking after them so well.

With love from your affectionate uncle,

Morton

Dear Uncle Morton,

Will you please send me some pictures of the footprints? I've always wanted to see a yeti.

If you find one, will you bring it home? Do you think it will be friends with the dragons?

They're both fine, by the way.

We had fish sticks for dinner. Arthur ate seven, and Ziggy had nine. Now they're dozing in front of the TV.

Mom would like to know when you're planning to come and get them. She says it's very nice having the dragons stay, but she'd like to have the house to herself again.

I think she's just feeling a bit grumpy because Gordon's gone home. Apparently, they had the best time ever in Paris.

Emily asked if we could go next time, too, and Mom said, "We'll see."

I'm feeling a bit grumpy, too, because I had to go back to school today.

It was okay, but being on vacation was much more fun.

Love,

Eddie

P.S. The egg still hasn't hatched. I've put it back in my sock drawer for now.

GREETINGS FROM TIBET

POSTCARD

Dear Eddie,

Yesterday we spotted a yeti!

We are going after him today.

Love,

Uncle Morton

Eddie

29 Po

She

W

What's next for Eddie, Ziggy & Arthur?

Don't miss their seventh adventure!

Turn the page for a sneak peek.

COMING SOON

Dear Uncle Morton,

Can I borrow your dragons?

Next week there is a costume competition at the Halloween Parade.

The first-place prize is a new computer, which is exactly what we need.

Our computer is Dad's old one. He left it behind when he moved out, and that was four years ago. It was already ancient then.

Also, Emily spilled a glass of milk on the keyboard and now the keys only work if you press them really hard.

All our problems would be solved if we won that prize.

Unfortunately, we don't have very good costumes.

I was planning to go as Frankenstein's monster, but I can't find any bolts for my neck.

Emily wants to be a ghost, but that just means wearing a sheet and going "Whoooo, whoooo" and she's never going to win anything for that.

Could we borrow your dragons?

With them we'd be sure to win first place.

We would only actually need Ziggy and Arthur
for one night, but Mom says you are welcome
to stay for the whole week, as long as you don't
mind sleeping on the sofa.

Granny is staying for fall break, and I bet
she would really like to see you, too.

Love from your favorite nephew,

Eddie

Dear Eddie,

I would have loved to join you for Halloween. There are few things that I like more than tricks and treats. Sadly, though, I must stay here in Scotland because I am hard at work preparing for my trip to Oregon in search of Bigfoot.

However, Gordon has kindly volunteered to come in my place. I think he just wants an excuse to see your mother. He is always complaining about how much he misses her.

As you will see for yourself, Arthur is going through a growth spurt at the moment and hasn't quite mastered the art of breathing fire. You may want to keep an extinguisher handy.

Thank you for the picture of your costumes. You both look lovely, but I can see why you need a little help. I'm sure the dragons will be just the ticket. If they aren't, perhaps you could persuade your mother to buy you a new computer? Or a second-hand one? Surely they aren't too expensive these days.

What a pity that I will not get to see my own mother. But please do send Granny my best wishes.

With love from your affectionate uncle,

Morton

Dear Uncle Morton,

Thank you very much for sending the dragons with Gordon.

I promise we will take very good care of them.

I know we've had a few disasters before, but this time will be different.

I just hope we win first place. The computer isn't going to live much longer. It keeps moaning and groaning, and the screen has gone wobbly.

I asked Mom if she could buy us a new one, but she said single-parent families can't afford luxuries like brand-new computers.

She said even a second-hand one would be too much for us in the current economic climate.

I asked what the current economic climate was, and she said gloomy.

Love,

Eddie

Dear Uncle Morton,

Do you like our tam-o'-shanters?

Gordon gave them to me and Emily. He says we look like proper wee Scots.

He also brought lots of presents for Mom. We just ate some of the smoked salmon with our scrambled eggs.

Mom said it was the most delicious breakfast of her entire life, and I think it might have been mine, too.

I see what you mean about Arthur breathing fire. He's already had a few accidents. But Mom said it didn't matter.

I think she's just happy to see Gordon.

Also, he peed on the carpet. (Arthur, I mean, not Gordon.) But you can't blame him for that. He must have been desperate after driving all the way from Scotland.

When everyone has recovered, we're going to make our costumes.

I've changed my mind about Frankenstein's monster. I'm going to be an Egyptian mummy instead.

Emily is still planning to go as a ghost, and the dragons can just be themselves.

I'll send you lots of pictures.

Love,

Eddie

Dear Uncle Morton,

We have a big problem, and we need your help.

This afternoon, Gordon asked Mom to marry him.

Obviously that's not the problem. We all really like Gordon. Especially Mom.

The problem is he got down on one knee and pulled a ring from his pocket.

Then he said, "Will you marry me?"

Mom literally couldn't speak.

If only she had said "yes" right away.

Then Gordon could have put the ring on her finger and everything would have been fine.

Unfortunately, Mom just stood there with her mouth open, staring at the ring as if she'd never seen anything like it before.

Which gave Arthur enough time to fly across the room and snatch it out of Gordon's hand.

I don't know why he did that. I've never eaten a ring myself, but I can't imagine it's very tasty.

Even so, he swallowed it quicker than you could say "I do."

Mom and Gordon tried to force Arthur's mouth open and pull the ring right out again, which wasn't exactly smart.

Gordon is very upset. Not just about his burned fingers, but also about the ring.

It belonged to his great-aunt Isla. She wore it every day for sixty-seven years.

Now it's inside Arthur's tummy, and we don't know how to get it out.

Do you have any brilliant ideas?

Love,

Eddie

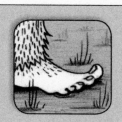
Dear Eddie,

I'm terribly sorry to hear about Gordon's great-aunt's ring.

Unfortunately, I can't imagine any way to extract it from Arthur's stomachs. (As you will remember from reading my book, dragons have three.)

If I were you, I would simply keep Arthur indoors for the next couple of days. The ring is sure to progress steadily through his guts and emerge eventually in his poop. Make sure you check them thoroughly. Once you have washed the ring, it will be as good as new, if not even better.

To speed up the process, you could feed him some dried fruit. Figs or apricots would be perfect.

Don't forget to keep all your doors and windows firmly closed. All would be lost if Arthur was allowed to leave the house and take flight. You would never find the ring again if he pooped in midair.

On a quite different subject, please share my congratulations with Gordon and your mother.

I hope they don't mind, but I have already announced the good news to Gordon's uncle, Mr. McDougall. Tonight we had drink together in celebration.

Is Gordon planning to move south? Or are you all going to come and live in Scotland? I hope you do. I couldn't imagine having nicer neighbors than you and Emily.

With love from your affectionate uncle,

Morton

Dear Uncle Morton,

I asked Mom if we were moving to Scotland or staying here, and she said she hasn't had a moment to think about the wedding, let alone where we're going to live.

Mostly she's been worrying about how to get the ring out of Arthur.

She said she was going to kill him. I am almost sure she was joking. Even so, I locked him in the oven.

He didn't seem to mind. He just curled up and went to sleep.

I think he must have known it was for his own safety.

I would have liked to have kept him in there until he pooped, but we're having baked potatoes for lunch.

Mom said turning the oven on would be fine, Arthur or no Arthur, but Gordon wasn't sure that was such a good idea.

I don't think he was too concerned about Arthur's personal safety. He just thought Arthur might explode, taking the ring with him.

So now he's in a cardboard box on the kitchen floor.

Love,

Eddie

Dear Uncle Morton,

Mom says we can't go to the Halloween Parade unless we get the ring out of Arthur.

I asked why not, and she said we have to understand that actions have consequences.

I said that's not fair because it wasn't me and Emily who swallowed the ring, but she said that's not the point.

I asked what was the point, and she said I should think about it.

I have been thinking about it. A lot. But I still don't know.

All I do know is this: if we are going to win that new computer, we have to get the ring out of Arthur.

THE DRAGONSITTER Series

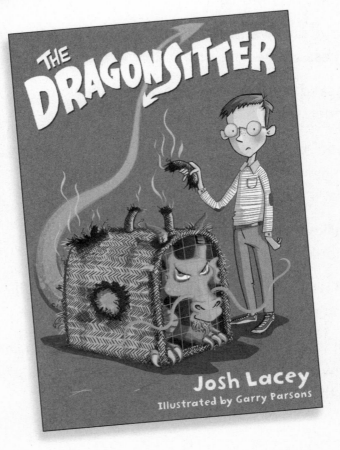

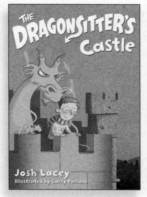

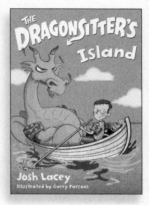

COLLECT THEM ALL!

If you enjoyed **THE DRAGONSITTER to the Rescue**, you might also like these series, available now!

GET READY TO GO INTERGALACTIC!

SPACE TAXI
ARCHIE'S ALIEN DISGUISE

SPACE TAXI
B.U.R.P. STRIKES BACK

SPACE TAXI
THE GALACTIC B.U.R.P.

SPACE TAXI
WATER PLANET RESCUE

SPACE TAXI
ARCHIE TAKES FLIGHT

The out-of-this-world series by
WENDY MASS
and
MICHAEL BRAWER

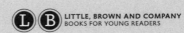

About the Author

JOSH LACEY is the author of many books for children, including *The Island of Thieves*, *Bearkeeper*, and the Grk series. He worked as a journalist, a teacher, and a screenwriter before writing his first book, *A Dog Called Grk*. Josh lives in London with his wife and daughters.

About the Illustrator

GARRY PARSONS has illustrated several books for children and is the author and illustrator of *Krong!*, winner of the Perth and Kinross Picture Book Award. Garry lives in London.